SWAT
Secret World Adventure Team

TOKYO TECHNO

by
Lisa Thompson

illustrated by
Jimmy Chan

PICTURE WINDOW BOOKS
Minneapolis, Minnesota

Editor: Jill Kalz
Page Production: Tracy Kaehler
Creative Director: Keith Griffin
Editorial Director: Carol Jones

First American edition published in 2006 by
Picture Window Books
5115 Excelsior Boulevard
Suite 232
Minneapolis, MN 55416
877-845-8392
www.picturewindowbooks.com

First published in Australia by
Blake Education Pty Ltd
CAN 074 266 023
Locked Bag 2022
Glebe NSW 2037
Ph: (02) 9518 4222; Fax: (02) 9518 4333
Email: mail@blake.com.au
www.askblake.com.au
© Blake Publishing Pty Ltd Australia 2005

Printed in the United States of America.

Library of Congress Cataloging-in-Publication Data
Thompson, Lisa, 1969–
Tokyo techno / by Lisa Thompson ; illustrated by Jimmy Chan.
p. cm. — (Read-it! chapter books. SWAT)
Summary: Jason and Anita are recruited by the Secret World
Adventure Team for a mission in Tokyo, where they learn a great
deal about Japanese culture while looking for the man they are
supposed to help debug a new computer game.
ISBN 1-4048-1673-9 (hardcover)
[1. Adventure and adventurers—Fiction. 2. Computer games—Fiction.
3. Tokyo (Japan)—Fiction. 4. Japan—Fiction.] I. Chan, Jimmy, ill.
II. Title. III. Series.
PZ7.T371634Tok 2005
[E]—dc22   2005027169

Table of Contents

MISSION No 0004

SWAT

DESTINATION PROFILE

* DESTINATION: Tokyo City Japan
* POPULATION: 8.3 million
* LANDMARKS Tokyo tower
  Mt. Fuji , Imperial P
  Shinto shrine. Nation
* Hottest weather in July
* Coldest weather in December
  Currency Yen
  Main
  Transport Train

入場書

NOH THEATER

F TOKYO

Shint
shrin

Mt.
Fuji

Mt. Fuji 富士山

S.W.A.T. ID
AGENT
CODE

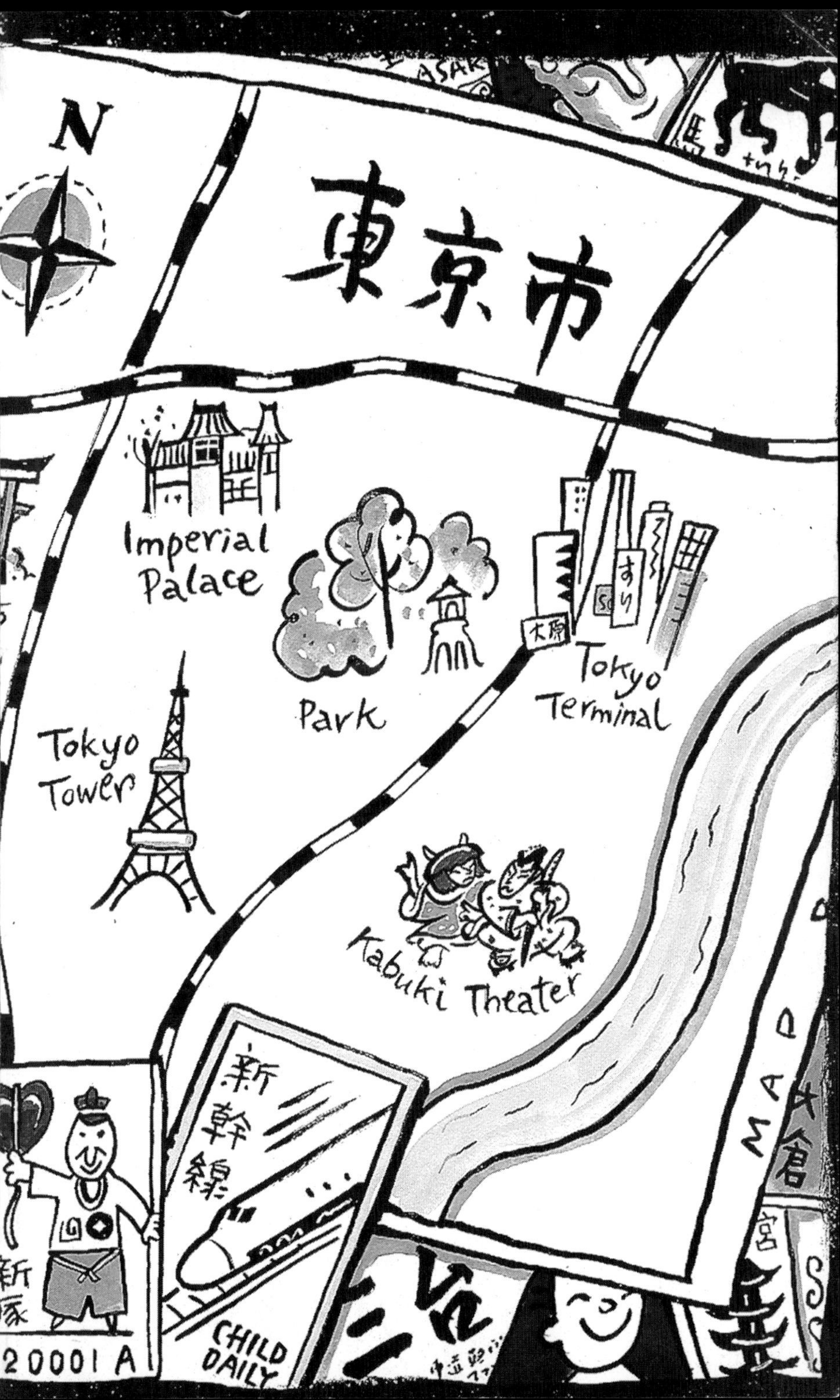
N
東京市
Imperial Palace
Park
Tokyo Terminal
Tokyo Tower
Kabuki Theater
新幹線
MAP
CHILD DAILY
20001 A

CHAPTER 1
THE MISSION

"Cool! I blasted you away!" said Jason.

"I'll get you. Just wait!" cried Anita.

BOOM! KAPOW! KAPOW!

"Game over, and I win again!" Jason said. "I am Jason, the computer game legend, master of any game."

"You wish! Let's play another game and see who wins," challenged Anita.

"Anita, you're my best friend. I'd hate to beat you AGAIN," said Jason. Just as Jason was about to turn off the computer, the screen started to flash.

"Who is SWAT?" asked Jason. He clicked on the mouse, and a voice came from the computer:

"Greetings, Jason and Anita. I am the voice of SWAT. My name is Gosic. SWAT is a top secret team whose name stands for Secret World Adventure Team. We have a database of every child in the world. From it we choose our special agents. You have been chosen for our next mission. We urgently need your help in Tokyo, Japan.

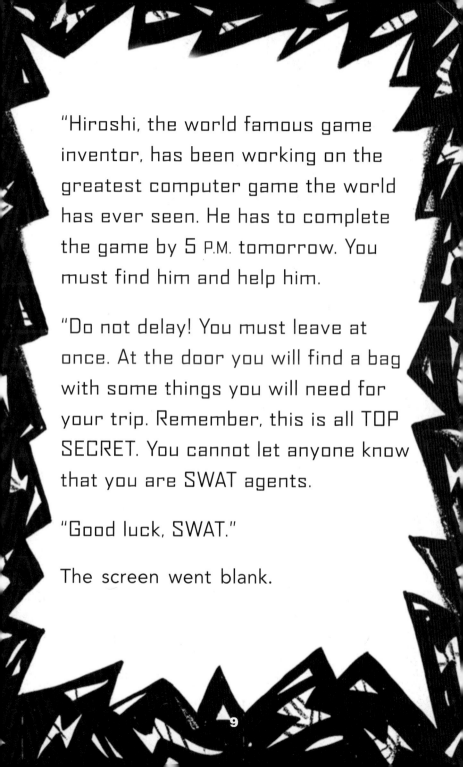

"Hiroshi, the world famous game inventor, has been working on the greatest computer game the world has ever seen. He has to complete the game by 5 P.M. tomorrow. You must find him and help him.

"Do not delay! You must leave at once. At the door you will find a bag with some things you will need for your trip. Remember, this is all TOP SECRET. You cannot let anyone know that you are SWAT agents.

"Good luck, SWAT."

The screen went blank.

Anita unzipped the bag.

"What is all of this stuff?" she asked.

Jason unfolded the map of the world.
Japan was circled.

"Japan isn't very big, is it?" Anita said, as she stared at the map.

"No, and it's a long way from here," said Jason.

Anita unfolded a map of Japan and started reading. "It says Japan is made up of four main islands and more than 3,000 little ones. The capital of Japan is Tokyo. That's where we're going." Anita marked Tokyo, on the island of Honshu, with a red circle.

Jason pointed to a white flag with a red circle in the middle. "That's the Japanese flag," he said. "The word 'Japan' means 'beginning of the sun.'"

"How do you know that?" asked Anita, sounding surprised.

"I saw it on the Internet," said Jason.

"Check this out!" said Anita, holding up some Japanese money.

"That's yen," said Jason. "My dad always tells me when the value of the yen goes up or down. He's into all of that money market stuff."

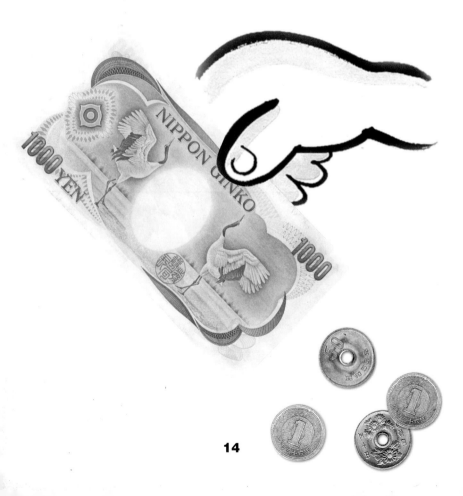

Anita wasn't listening. She was working her way through a book of Japanese words and phrases.

"The Japanese language is totally different than English," she said. "*Konnichiwa* means 'good afternoon.' *Sayonara* means 'good-bye.' *Hai* is 'yes,' and *arigato* is 'thank you.'"

長年医者をやっていると、この人の病気が合うやすいか治りにくいかはすぐにわかる。

Jason tried saying a sentence in Japanese. He wanted to say, "This mission sounds like fun." But he got it wrong and said, "Help me! I have a toothache!"

Anita started to laugh, but she stopped when Jason pulled a strange, black box out of the bag.

"Now, this looks interesting," she said.

Inside the box were two wristbands.
They were marked:

SWAT transporter wristbands—
MUST BE WORN AT ALL TIMES

"The instructions say that wearing these lets Gosic contact us. The wristbands also allow us to go places in the blink of an eye," he said.

"Well, let's go!" said Anita.

They counted down together—"Three, two, one"—and pushed the button marked **START MISSION**.

Click.

START MISSION.

CHAPTER 2
TOKYO WITH TOSHI

They were both suddenly standing on a street corner in the heart of Tokyo.

"Look out!" cried Anita, as she pulled Jason out of the way of a sea of people about to cross the road.

"How many people live in this place?"
asked Anita. "This city is packed!"

Jason opened his fact book. "It says
here that more than 125 million people
live in Japan. More than 8 million
people live in Tokyo."

21

"Check out the buildings on this street!" cried Anita in amazement. "These skyscrapers look like they go on forever!"

"Let's go find Hiroshi," said Jason.

The two friends went to catch a taxi. The streets were blocked with traffic. At the taxi stand, people were very polite as Anita tried to speak Japanese. They smiled and bowed. Jason and Anita smiled and bowed back.

A girl walked up and tapped Jason on the shoulder. She had black hair and a beautiful smile. It looked like everyone in Tokyo had black hair.

"Welcome to Tokyo!" said the girl. "My name is Toshi, and I am the best travel guide in Japan. It would be my pleasure to show you around."

Before they could say a word, Toshi
had them in a taxi. She pointed to the
sights and reeled off facts. They tried
to keep up with her, but she was
making their heads spin.

"So many cars!" said Jason, looking out each of the taxi's windows.

"Japan is one of the largest carmakers in the world," Toshi said proudly. "We export our cars everywhere!"

The taxi stopped at the
Japanese gardens, and they
got out to see the cherry
blossoms. The garden was
full of people eating and
drinking beneath the trees.

"Lots of people come here to celebrate the birth of the new spring season," said Toshi, leading the way.

"What happened to that tree? It looks like it's been shrunk!" cried Anita.

"That's a Bonsai tree. Keeping it small is an ancient Japanese art," Toshi said.

BONSAI 盆栽

The trio walked through the crowded streets to a Shinto shrine.

"What are all of these pieces of paper with writing on them?" asked Jason.

"That's how people tell their prayers and wishes to the gods," Toshi explained. "They write them down."

Toshi led them through the shrine. She quietly pointed out the statues of different gods and lit some incense.

"Enough sightseeing for now," she said, once they were outside again. "It is time for you to have a real Tokyo experience."

Before they could blink, Toshi had them on a crowded train platform. It was rush hour, and everyone was going to work. A train pulled up right away. They got on, and to their amazement, so did everyone else.

There were people on the platform called "pushers." Their job was to squeeze as many people as they could into each train car.

"Jason, I can't move my arms!" Anita whispered. "How about you?"

"I'm totally squashed," moaned Jason.

"In Japan, people work very long hours, and almost everyone rides the train. Ohhhh, look at that billboard!" Toshi exclaimed.

Jason and Anita could barely turn their heads. They were squished between a huge sumo wrestler and a girl wearing a kimono.

Jason caught a glimpse of the billboard. It read:

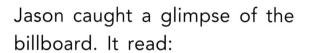

Hiroshi, master game inventor! New game launched worldwide on the Internet tomorrow, 5 P.M.

"I sure hope so," thought Jason.

As they got off the train, Jason whispered, "Anita, we really have to lose this girl and find Hiroshi."

Toshi pointed them toward another train.

"No way, Toshi. Not another train ride,"
Anita said, waving her hands.

34

"This train is a bullet train. It goes very fast. Hurry, we'll be back before you know it," said Toshi.

Jason took out the fact book and looked up "bullet train." He read, "Can travel at speeds of up to 170 miles (275 kilometers) per hour. OK, one quick trip, and then we have to go."

As they sped through the countryside,
Anita asked, "Do the bullet trains
always go this fast?"

"Most of the time," said Toshi, "except
when there is an earthquake warning.
Then the trains slow down to be safe."

"Earthquakes!" said Jason.

"Yes," said Toshi, "Japan has about four earthquakes a day, but few are ever felt."

"I think I feel one now," joked Anita, bouncing up and down on her seat.

富士山 Mt. Fuji

Mt. Fuji last erupted in 1707

Jason looked out the window. Beyond the rice fields he could see a huge, snow-capped mountain. "That mountain looks like an old volcano," he said.

"It is. Japan is full of volcanoes," said Toshi. "That's Mount Fuji, Japan's most famous mountain."

Jason pulled out an instant camera and took a photo. On the bottom of the photo he wrote, "Mount Fuji, Japan—famous old volcano."

When the train arrived back at the station, Jason and Anita planned a quick exit.

"Thanks, Toshi, we have to go now. We have something very important we must do," said Jason.

Time was ticking away, and they hadn't even started to look for Hiroshi.

"No, wait! There is still so much more to see and do!" Toshi protested, as she dragged them down a path filled with paper lanterns. Inside one doorway was a kendo class.

Next door, a traditional Japanese Kabuki play was being performed.

"What is this play about?" asked Jason.

"It's the story of two samurai," said Toshi. "Samurai are Japanese warriors. They are highly skilled fighters who live by a very strict code. The play tells of the courage of the two samurai as they avenge their father's death. The play goes on all day, and you can come and go as you please."

They hurried off down a street strung with paper birds. Toshi showed them how to make one by folding paper.

"We call this paper-folding art form origami," she explained.

They stopped and listened to an old man reciting Japanese haiku poems. Toshi told them how to create one. Anita thought they sounded great and tried to make one up.

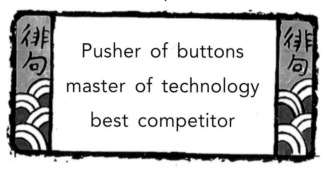

Pusher of buttons
master of technology
best competitor

"Great effort!" said Jason. "Love it. Now, let's get going."

"Wait!" said Anita, "I have to buy one of these dragon kites."

"And I have to get some of these," said Jason, running into a shop. He couldn't believe how many gadgets and games there were. "This has to be technology heaven," he said.

"Check your fact book!" laughed Anita.

"Japan makes more electronic goods than any other country in the world," Jason read. "Look at that high-definition TV ... and listen to the sound on this CD player ... just look how tiny and fast this computer is ... man, I can't believe this place!"

長年医者の心の持ちそれは病気治りやすい

As Jason looked around the store, he noticed a giant poster in the window. It said, "Hiroshi's new game launch— 5 P.M. tomorrow."

"Looks like everyone's waiting for this game," he whispered to Anita.

They walked out into the busy street.

"You must see this!" said Toshi, dragging them inside a theater. "It's an old Japanese movie about a monster dinosaur called Godzilla."

Jason was getting even more impatient. He shook his head and said, "I'm sorry, Toshi, we can't. We really have to go. You see we ...."

"But you can't go yet. You haven't had anything to eat," Toshi said.

It was getting late, and they were really hungry. Toshi led them to a restaurant. They took off their shoes, slid on slippers, and sat on cushions at a low table.

"Eat oodles of noodles with your chopsticks, and try the sushi," said the waiter.

"What's sushi?" Anita asked the waiter.

"Sushi is raw fish with rice," he replied.

うどん Noodle

すし SUSHI

After dinner, Toshi, Jason, and Anita sipped on green tea and sang karaoke.

Jason tried again. "Toshi, we are having a great time, but Anita and I really do have to go."

"Wait! There is my uncle. You must meet him," said Toshi, grabbing a short, round man. He had been singing karaoke very badly into a microphone.

"Jason and Anita, this is my uncle Hiroshi—Master Game Inventor!"

Jason and Anita were stunned. This was the man they had to find!

At that moment, a message appeared on their wristbands:

HURRY, SWAT!
TIME IS
RUNNING OUT!

CHAPTER 5
HIROSHI'S GAME

"It's an honor to meet you, Mr. Hiroshi," said Anita with a bow.

"We can't wait to play your new game. It sounds very exciting," said Jason.

"Oh, yes it is," said Hiroshi wearily.

"You sure don't sound very excited,"
said Jason.

"Oh, I am," said Hiroshi, not very
convincingly. "It's just that it's not
really finished. There seems to be a
little problem." He quickly changed the
subject. "I love singing," he continued.
"It takes my mind off things."

"But you sing so badly," said Anita without thinking.

"Oh, I know!" said Hiroshi with a smile on his face.

"You really do need to finish your project," said Jason. "Maybe we could help you with it."

"How?" asked Hiroshi, raising an eyebrow in interest.

"It just so happens that Anita and I are experts at playing computer games," Jason explained.

Hiroshi didn't look convinced.

"Jason's a great singer, too! I bet he could give you some singing lessons afterward," said Anita.

"I am? I could?" said Jason.

"Oh, that sounds wonderful!" cried Hiroshi enthusiastically. "I have a few favorites I've been wanting to learn. Quickly, we must leave now. We don't have a lot of time."

The trio left Toshi singing her favorite song and headed for Hiroshi's home.

Hiroshi lived in a small apartment not far from the restaurant. It was packed from floor to ceiling with every modern electronic gadget and game ever invented. Hiroshi, singing away, started setting things up.

"I know I've made many games, but this is definitely the greatest game I have ever come up with. I want you to play it and tell me what you think. Here, put these on." Hiroshi handed them robes similar to the one he was wearing. "These are *yukata*. They are very comfortable."

Jason and Anita put them on and agreed with Hiroshi; the yukata were very comfortable.

Hiroshi led them through the game, explaining how it all worked and how to play.

"Awesome!" declared Jason. "This game is a million times better than anything I have ever played!"

"There is one small problem," said Hiroshi, lowering his voice. "The game has a virus in it that corrupts all other games on your computer. It destroys them. I have tried to fix the problem, but it seems impossible!"

"And the whole world is waiting for the game to be launched tomorrow," said Jason.

CHAPTER 6
FIXING THE GAME

"This game wipes out every other computer game?" asked Anita.

Jason and Anita thought of all of their favorite games.

"That would be a disaster!" said Jason.

"It will be if we can't fix it by 5 P.M. tomorrow," said Hiroshi.

"What are we standing around for?" cried Jason. "Let's get to work! Hiroshi, show me the program. Anita, set the game up on that computer there and that one there. We've got to fix this, and there's not a lot of time."

The three worked all through the night and the next day. It was tough going. Sometimes Hiroshi hummed a tune, but mostly they worked in silence. Jason and Anita tried everything they knew. Hiroshi wracked his brain. Could they fix the game before 5 P.M.?

9 PM • 10 PM • 11 PM • 12 PM • 1 am

Time ticked by. Five o'clock crept closer and closer.

2 am • 3 am • 4 am • 5 am • 6 am • 7 am • 8 am • 9 am • 10 am • 11 am • NOON • 1 PM • 2 PM • 3 PM • 4 PM • 5

12 noon.

2 P.M.

3 P.M.

4 P.M.

4:30 P.M.

Then, after much hard work, they did it. Success! They squealed and yelled for joy. They danced and sang.

Then Anita yelled, "Look at the time! Quickly, let's get it on the Internet."

The time was 4:58 P.M. They had beaten the deadline by TWO minutes!

Hiroshi started singing at the top of his lungs, shouting, "Brilliant! Fantastic! Absolutely amazing!"

Jason thought of all of the millions of people around the world playing Hiroshi's game that very second. He shook his head and said, "So close! Man, I can't believe it!"

"Thank you," beamed Hiroshi. "You are definitely computer legends!"

"Thanks," said Jason and Anita proudly.

At that moment, a message came up
on their wristbands:

MISSION SUCCESSFUL.

GREAT JOB, SWAT.

CONGRATULATIONS!

Immediately after that, a red button
appeared marked **MISSION RETURN**.

"And now we will begin the singing lessons. Wait here while I pick my favorite songs," Hiroshi said, rushing next door.

"I can't believe what we just did! It was awesome!" said Anita, still beaming. "When I tell—"

"Remember what Gosic said? We can't tell anyone about SWAT," Jason said.

"Oh, relax, Jason. No one would believe us anyway!"

They both laughed.

"What kind of mission do you think Gosic has in store for the next SWAT team?" Anita asked.

"I don't know, but they can call me back anytime," Jason said. "That was the coolest thing I have ever done! Quick, let's head home before Hiroshi comes back for those lessons."

東京さよなら
SAYONARA
TO
TOKYO

"Do you think your mom would make us some sushi when we get back? I'm so hungry!" Anita said.

"I'm sure she'll have some raw fish and seaweed for you somewhere," laughed Jason. "Now, let's go home! Three. Two. One."

Click.

MISSION RETURN.

GLOSSARY

arigato—(a-ree-ga-toh) Japanese for "thank you"

avenge—to make someone pay for a wrong he or she has done

convincingly—very believably

export—to sell to another country

hai—(hi) Japanese for "yes"

haiku—a three-line Japanese poem in which the first and third lines have five syllables and the second line has seven syllables

Kabuki—a form of Japanese theater

karaoke—singing along to a video clip that plays the music and shows the words

kendo—a style of sword fighting using bamboo sticks

kimono—a traditional Japanese robe

konnichiwa—(koh-nee-chee-wah) Japanese for "good afternoon"

origami—the Japanese fine art of folding paper

rush hour—the time of the day when the traffic is the busiest

sayonara—(sa-yoh-na-ra) Japanese for "good-bye"

Shinto shrine—a place of worship

sumo wrestler—a wrestler who uses his huge body to push his opponent

sushi—food made of raw fish, rice, and seaweed

yukata—an informal, lightweight Japanese robe

竜記念
ssion Ticket

The Donjon(main structure)reflects 16th centu... architectural influences.

IWAKUNI CASTLE

...an Rail Pa

真実の人生

・インフルエンザ
・痴呆老人の悩み
・健康・生かされ
・病気が治りやす

IT COULD BE YOU!

Secret World Adventure Team

COME
TRAVEL
TODAY!

A complete list of *Read-it!* Chapter Books is
available on our Web site:
www.picturewindowbooks.com